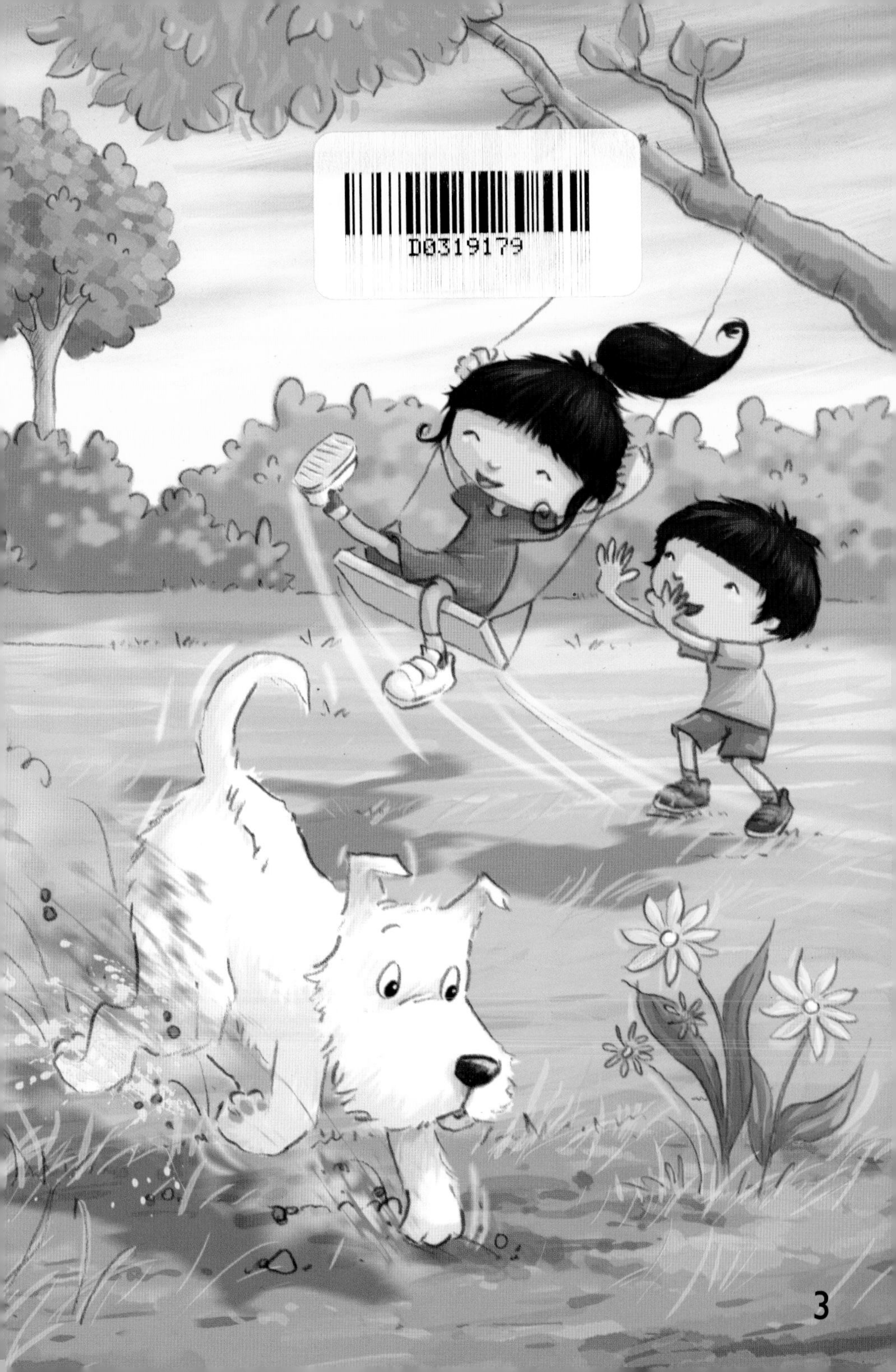

Dog likes to dig.

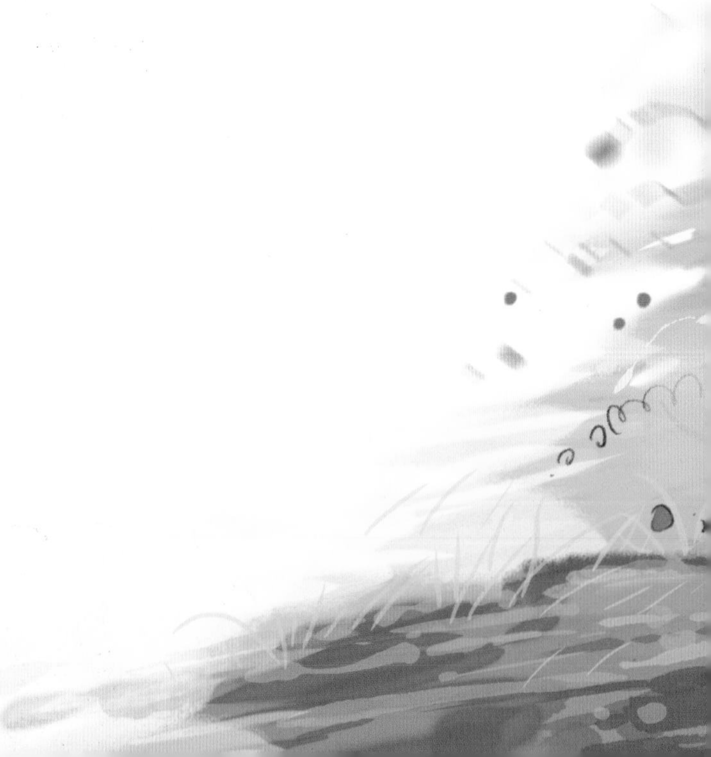

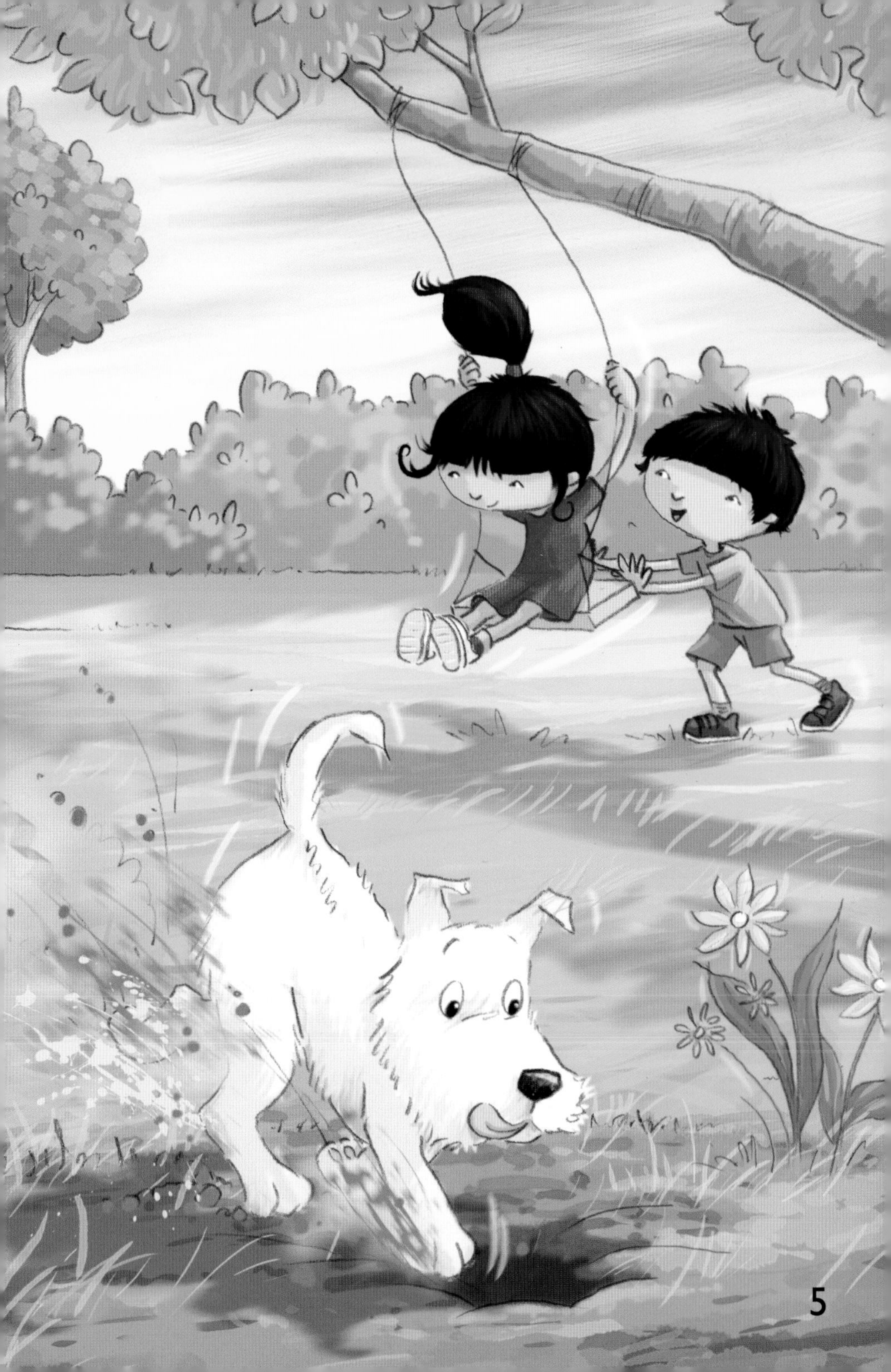

Dog likes to dig.

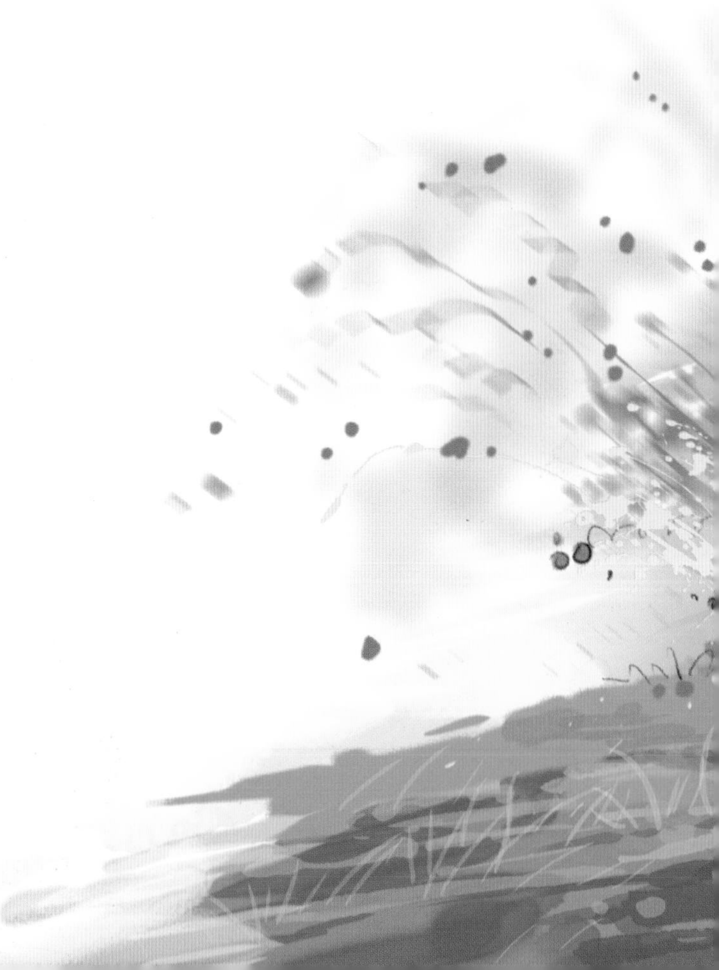

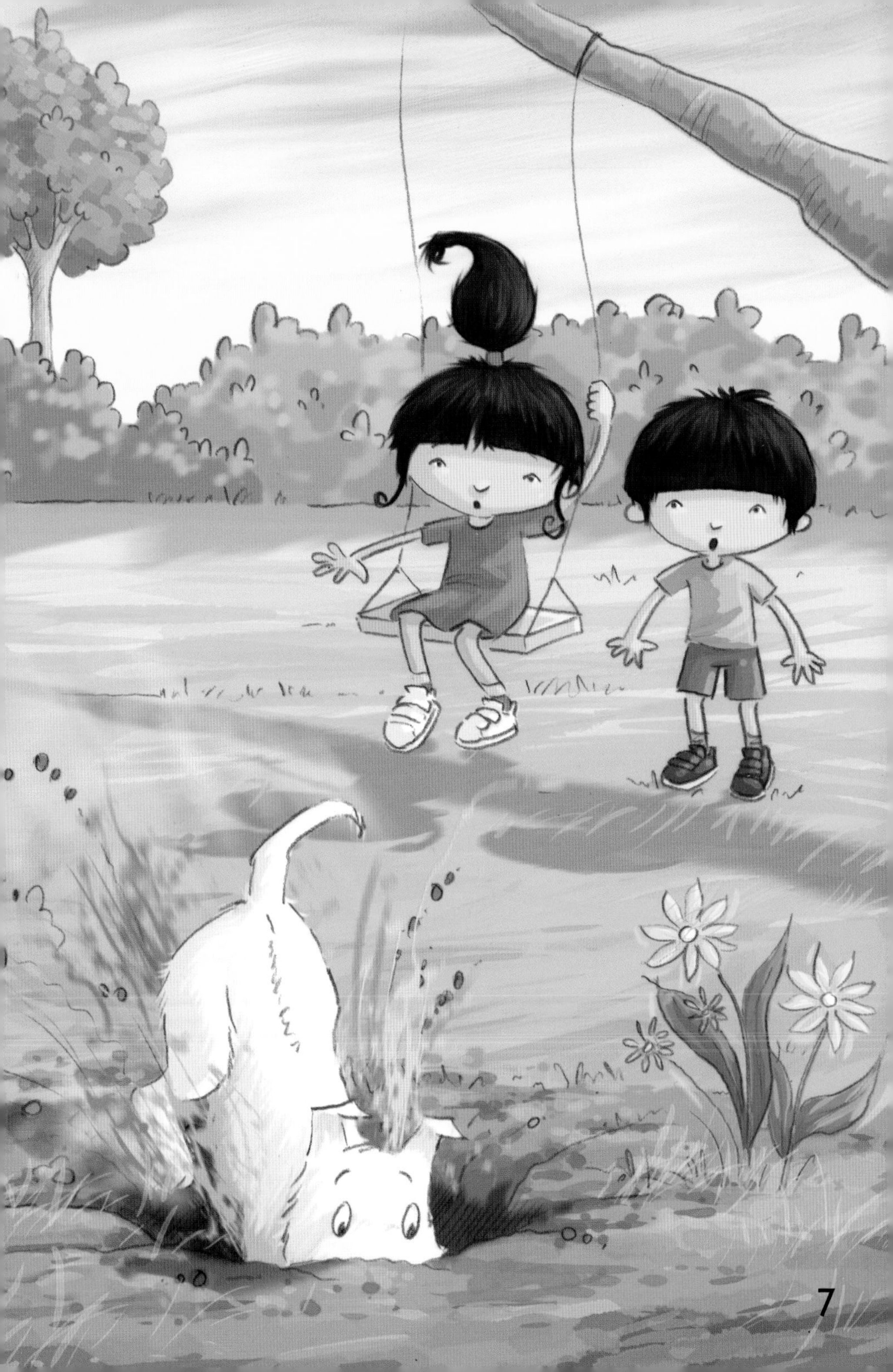

Dog likes to dig.

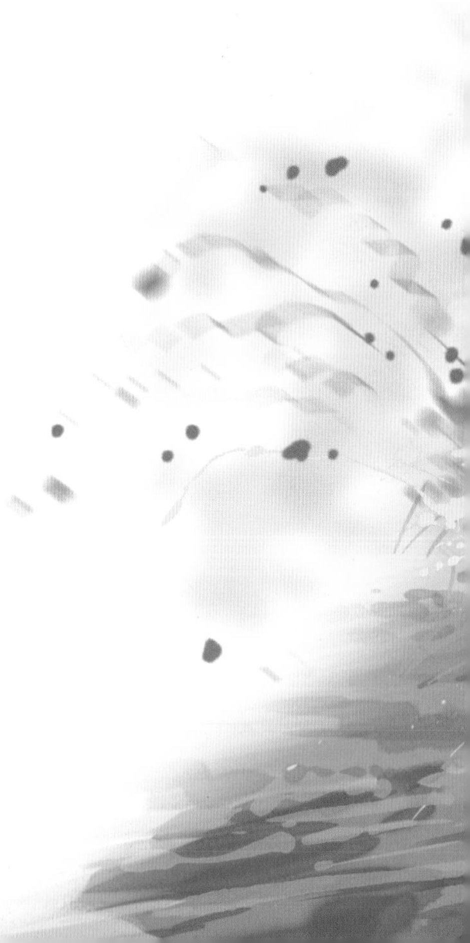

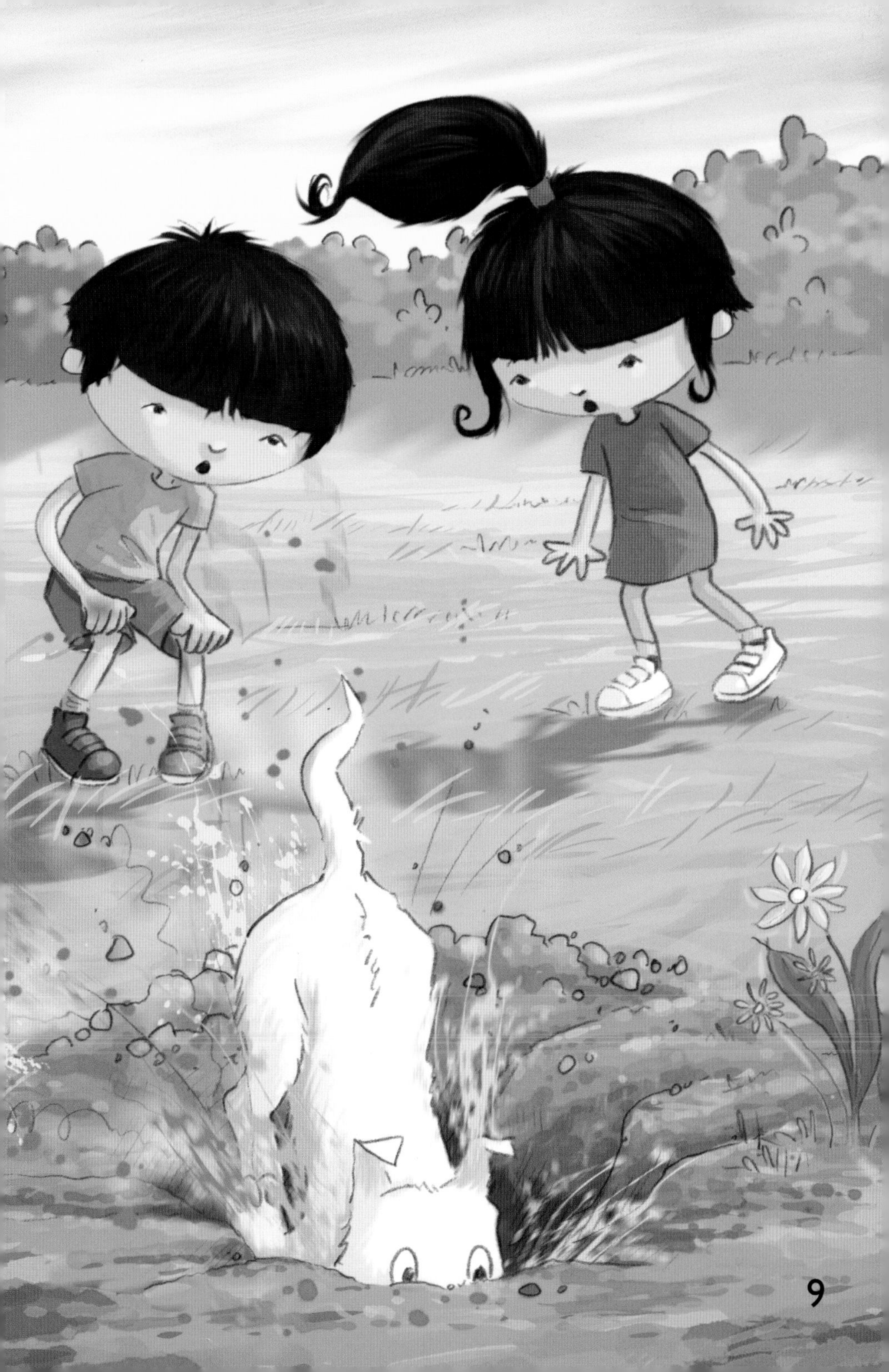

Dog likes to dig.

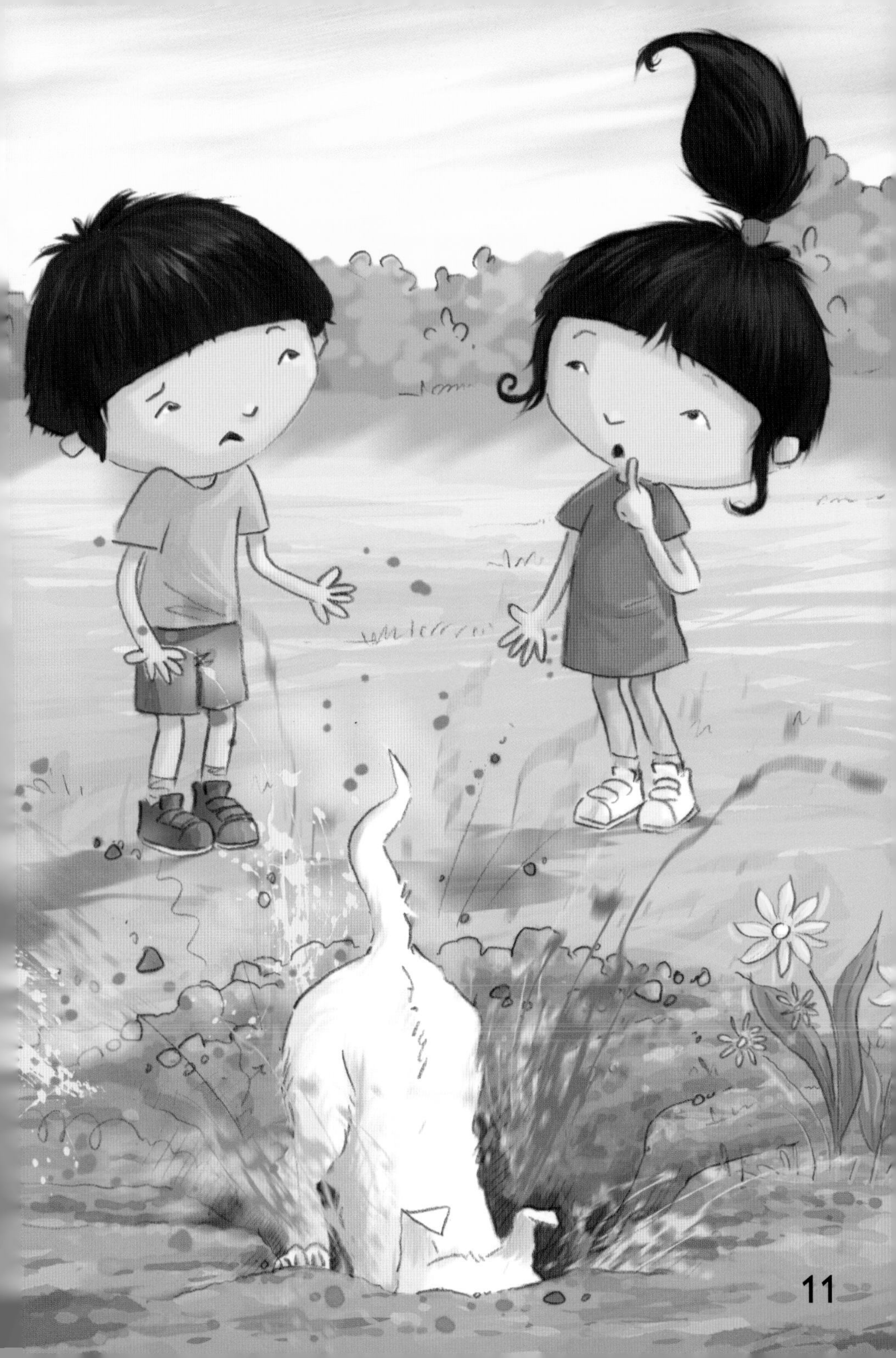

Dog likes to dig.

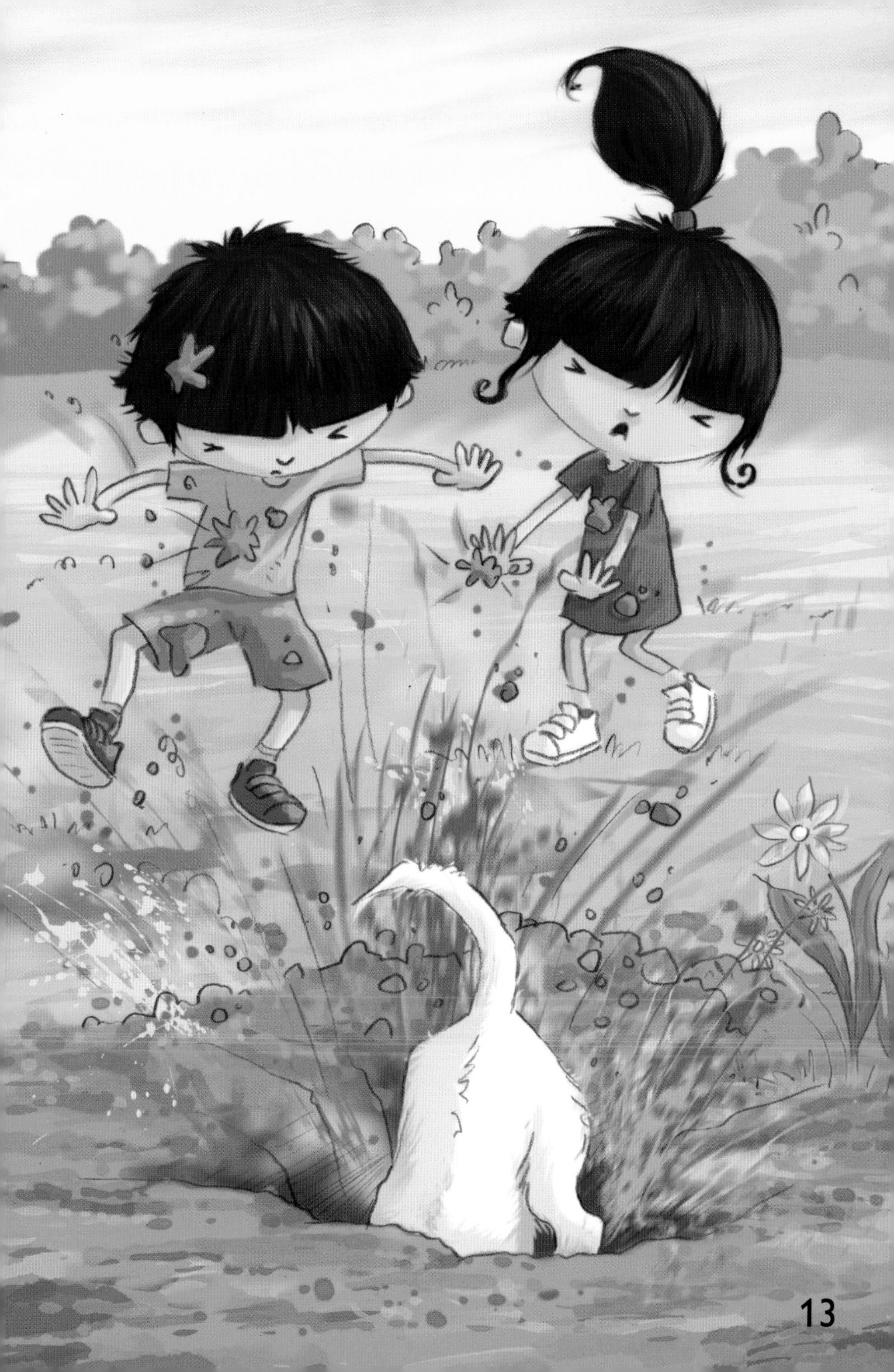

Dog likes to dig.

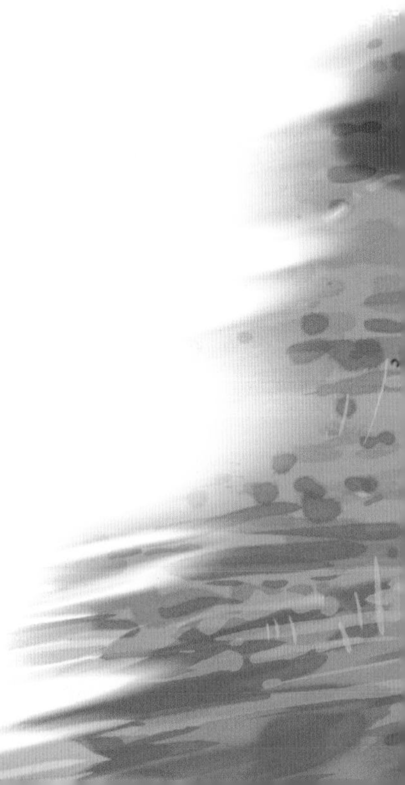

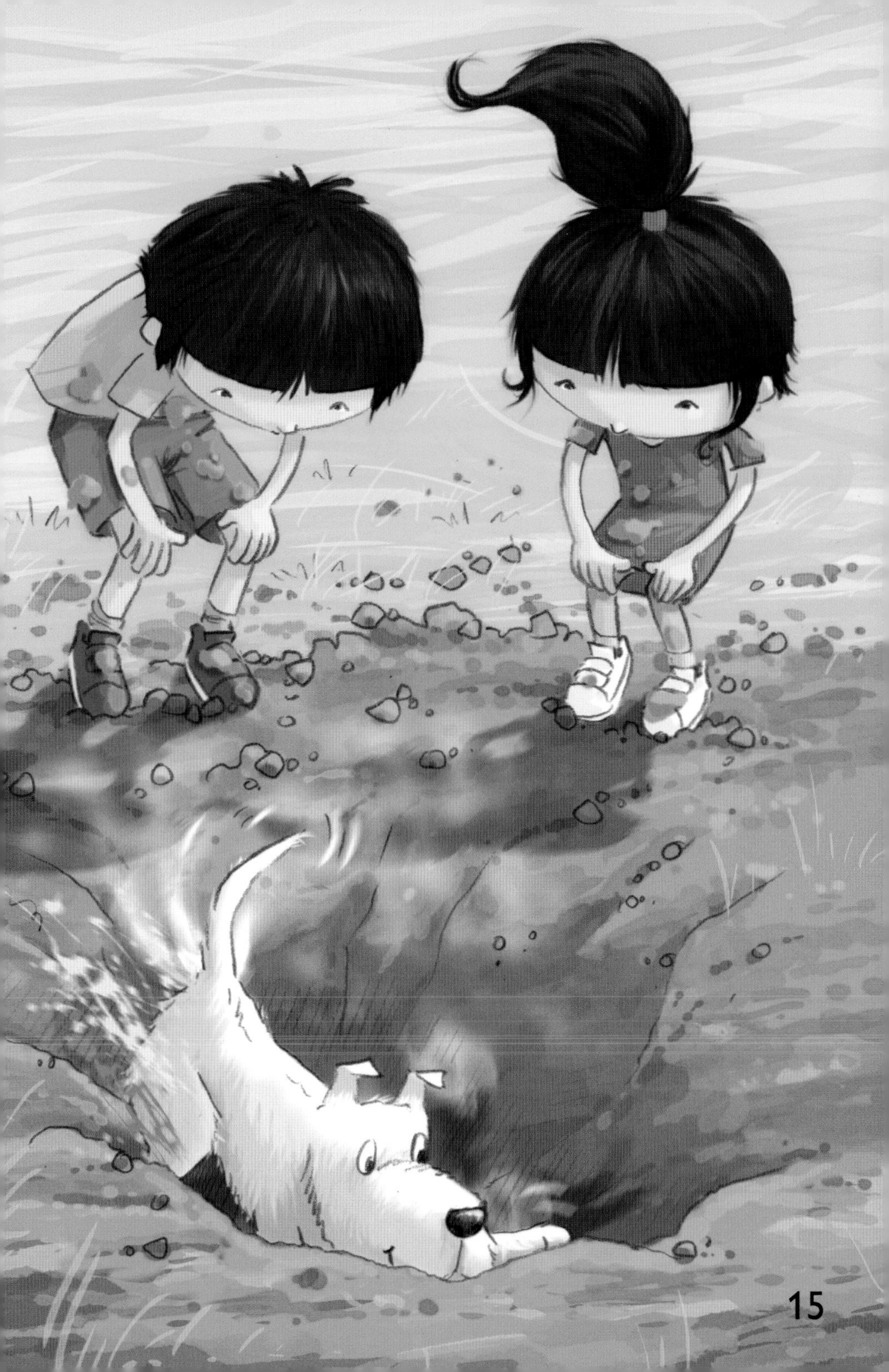

Dog likes to dig.

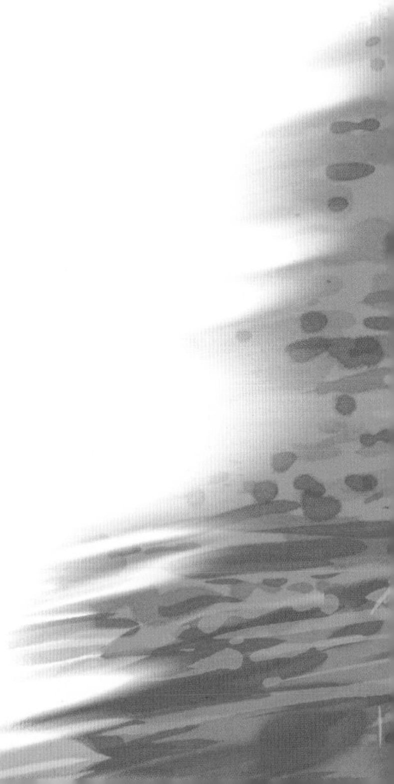

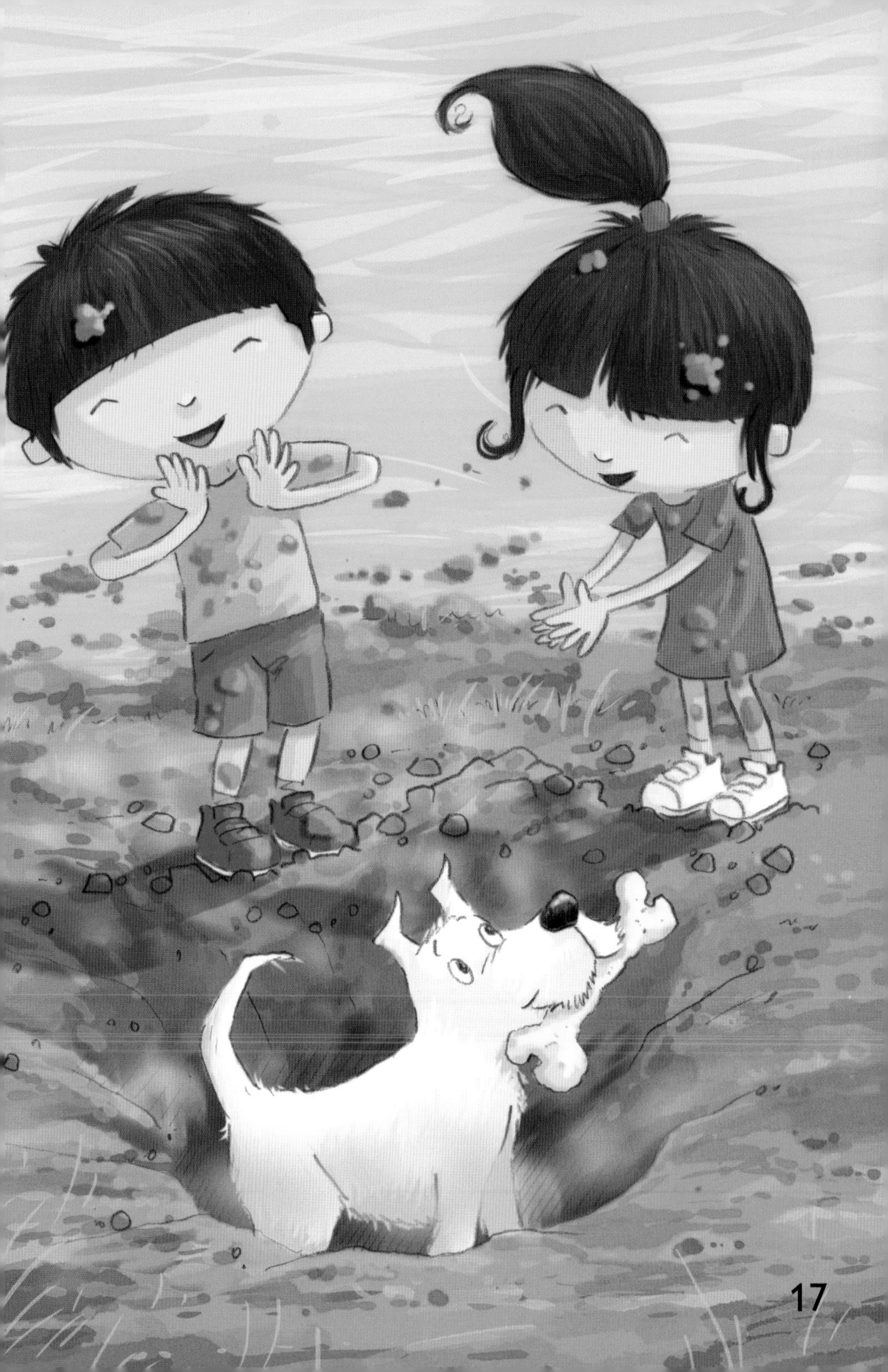

Dog likes to dig.